nterbury
Calais

Reims

is

Bar-sur-Aube

Besançon

Lausanne

San Bernard Pass

Aosta

Pavia

Castelletto

Marina di Carrara

Siena

Assisi

For my mother, and special thanks to Dott. Angelo Carzaniga
who first told me about the 'Via Francigena' – P.B.

For Tiziana – G.G.

First published in Great Britain in 1999 by Bloomsbury Publishing Plc
38 Soho Square, London W1V 5DF

Text copyright © Patricia Borlenghi 1999
Illustrations copyright © Giles Greenfield 1999
The moral right of the author has been asserted.

A CIP catalogue record for this book is available from the British Library.
ISBN 0 7475 4491 3

Designed by Dawn Apperley

Printed and bound at Oriental Press, Dubai

1 3 5 7 9 10 8 6 4 2

Chaucer the Cat
AND THE
ANIMAL PILGRIMS

Patricia Borlenghi and Giles Greenfield

BLOOMSBURY
CHILDREN'S
BOOKS

Introduction

This collection of animal stories is a unique commemoration of every pilgrimage that has taken place since the beginning of Christianity. In the year 2000 this ancient tradition will be restored with a pilgrimage to Rome. However in this book, the pilgrims are animals, who have gathered from all over the world to visit the site where St Francis of Assisi was buried.

The animals follow one of the real routes taken by Christian pilgrims over the last 2000 years. But the animals are going to Assisi rather than Rome, as St Francis of Assisi is the patron saint of animals. Many of the animals meet up in Paris at the Cathedral of Notre Dame. Chaucer the Cat has come from the City of London. Some animals, who have come from further afield, join the pilgrimage at other stages of the journey. They travel through the roads of France, Switzerland and Italy, some of which, even today, bear signs of the ancient pilgrimages. The route they follow is known historically as LA VIA FRANCIGENA. My ancestors came from Castelletto di Vernasca in Italy, which is along one of the many alternative trails which became known as part of 'la Via Francigena'. Loosely translated this means 'the French way'. The book includes a map which traces 'the French way' and indicates what stage the animals have reached on their journey.

As in Chaucer's Canterbury Tales, the stories are narrated by the animal pilgrims on their journey. It is the idea of Chaucer the Cat, who starts by telling a tale of his own. The other animals then each tell a story about their relationships with animals or humans. The stories are based on the writings of Aesop, La Fontaine and the brothers Grimm, and adapted from stories originating in Australia, Africa, North America, China, India and the West Indies. There is also a story about St Francis of Assisi, who was born in the twelvth century.

Each story is prefaced by a short description of each animal narrator, and the place where the animals have stopped on the route. The same stopping places have been used by pilgrims throughout the centuries.

This collection also celebrates the millennium, which, lest we forget, is the 2000th anniversary of the birth of Christ.

Patricia Borlenghi

CONTENTS

Chaucer the Cat

Many of the animals had arranged to meet at the famous cathedral of Notre Dame, in Paris. They had come from all over the world. The animals were going on a pilgrimage. They were making their way to the burial place of Saint Francis in Assisi, which is near Rome. They were going to honour Saint Francis, who is the patron saint of animals.

Soon the animals were on their way, and the line of animals stretched out very far, as far as the eye could see. It went up and down hills and along the banks of the River Seine, like a very long snake. They were journeying to the east of France and across the Alps from Switzerland into Italy. Other animals would be joining them on the route.

The way would be arduous and tiring. The road seemed never-ending and it would be many weeks before they reached Assisi.

Chaucer the Cat, was a magnificent grey tabby cat. He came from the city of London. From London he went to Canterbury and crossed the channel at Dover by ferry boat. He arrived at the port of Calais and from there had made his way to Paris. On the first night, the cathedral of Notre Dame could still be seen in the distance, and the animals were having their first rest period. Suddenly, Chaucer had a splendid idea. 'I know, let's tell stories to each other. This will make the time go quickly and we will all learn something. I propose that some of you volunteer to tell a story. But I'll go first — I will set the ball rolling ... I know a story called:

The Cat and the Mouse set up House

Once upon a time, a cat met a mouse, and a strange thing happened. They liked each other! So they decided to set up house together. The cat realised this would be a difficult thing, especially as the mouse was so small. 'We will have to store food for the winter. It would be very risky for you to go out seeking food, and, anyway, all the neighbours would talk about us! Who has ever heard of a cat and

mouse living together!

They decided to buy a pot of fish-oil but they did not know where to hide it. After a long discussion, they decided to hide it in the church.

'I can't think of anywhere safer than a church,' declared the cat. 'We'll hide it under the altar and we won't touch it until we need it.'

So they hid the pot in the church. But soon the cat felt a craving for it, and said to the mouse: 'I've been invited to a christening. My cousin has given birth to a baby boy, ever so sweet, a marmalade colour, and she has asked me to be one of the godparents. I'm afraid that you will have to stay here and do the housework by yourself.'

'Yes, of course,' said the mouse, 'off you go, and think of me when you are eating all those nice things and drinking that lovely red wine.'

But it was not true. The cat had no cousin, and there was no christening. The cat went straight to the church, up to the altar, and ate the top off the fish-oil. The cat then went for a walk on the rooftops, and stretched out in the sunshine, every

so often licking itself and wiping its whiskers, still thinking of the tasty oil. It was evening when the cat finally went home.

'Well,' said the mouse, 'I bet you had a good time.'

'Not bad,' said the cat.

'What name did they give the baby?' asked the mouse.

'Top-off,' said the cat quickly.

'What a strange name!' exclaimed the mouse.

'What's so strange about it,' said the cat defensively. 'It's no worse than being called Cheese-nibbler, like your godchild.'

It was not long before the cat had another craving. The cat said to the mouse: 'You'll have to do me another favour, and attend to the house yourself. I've been invited to another christening. I can't refuse — the baby has a white ring around its neck.'

The good mouse agreed and off the cat went back to the church, and this time, ate up half the fish-oil. The cat was very pleased with himself and returned home.

'What did they christen the child this time?' asked the mouse.

'Half-gone,' replied the cat.

'I've never heard such a name!' replied the mouse. 'I bet it's not in the Book of Saints.'

Soon the cat again began to hanker after the tasty oil.

'All things happen in threes,' the cat said to the mouse. 'I'm going to be a godparent again! You don't mind if I go out again?'

But the mouse was beginning to get suspicious. 'Top-off! Half-gone! Whatever next? Those names worry me,' said the mouse.

'Your problem is you don't get out enough,' replied the cat. 'You sit at home all day, getting moody, in your dark-grey coat and your pigtail...'

After the cat went out, the mouse tidied up the house and scrubbed everything clean. Meanwhile the greedy cat was finishing off the delicious fish-oil. 'Well, that's gone now. There's nothing left to worry about,' said the cat, stretching out. The cat's tummy was very full, and, that evening, he could barely manage to waddle off home.

The mouse asked straight away what name had been given to the child.

'You won't like it,' said the cat. 'The name is All-gone.'

'That's the worst name I've ever heard!' said the mouse. 'What can it mean?'

The cat shook its head, rolled up in a ball and went to sleep.

After that there were no more invitations to christenings for the cat. Winter came, and there was no food to be found, and the mouse remembered their pot of fish-oil.

'Come on, Cat,' said the mouse, 'let's go and get our secret supply of food in the church.'

'Oh yes, you'll enjoy it as much as tasting the cold night air,' said the cat, sarcastically.

Off they went to the church and the mouse went up to the altar and found the pot. But it was empty. Then it dawned on the mouse what had been happening.

'I see what you've been playing at. Some friend you turned out to be. First, Top-off, then Half-gone, and now All-gone.'

'Shut up,' said the cat, 'or you'll be All-gone too.'

The mouse ran out of the church and around the streets, chased by the cat.

'Well, that's the way things are. Cats and mice were never meant to be friendly!' announced Chaucer cheekily.

Dexter the Dog

Some of the animals cheered, others were not so sure, especially the mice in the party. Dexter the Dog barked excitedly. He had come all the way from the West Indies to join the pilgrimage. He was a big, beautiful black Labrador. He was clamouring to tell a story.

'Let me be next,' he said to Chaucer. 'I have a story about dogs from the beginning of time and why one thing is true about all dogs — a dog's nose is always cold.'

'Okay then, you can tell your story next,' said Chaucer. Now all the animals had something to look forward to, and the journey did not seem so long and wearisome after all.

The animals were well on their way now, and had stopped some way south of the French city of Reims. Many more animals coming from Germany, Eastern Europe and the East had travelled from Reims to meet the animals coming from Paris. Far in the distance, to the north, there was a huge cathedral and in the surrounding countryside were the vineyards where the famous Champagne grape was grown.

A Dog's Nose is Cold

After the flood, there was a shortage of food. Every morning Man looked towards the cloud-covered mountain and prayed to God to open the thick clouds and make the pink rocks shine with light. As he sowed his seeds, he prayed to God to warm the earth and to make his seeds grow.

This was the time when hungry Man first became a hunter. Craving for food, he looked for wild honey, but the bees were not making honey because the flood had destroyed the flowers. Man could not find fruits on the trees, because they too had been destroyed by the floods. Because Man could not find any fruit or honey, he set snares in the grass for the birds that made their nests there, and he made a bow with arrows to shoot the iguana, the armadillo and the wild pig. He went to the river and chose the longest, toughest canes that grew there. He made blowpipes for shooting the animals and he made spears by tipping the ends of some reeds with sharp bits of shell, bone or flint.

Armed with these weapons, Man went to the forest, but he did not know how to use the weapons very well and the animals remained unharmed. He missed the birds with his arrows, he broke his spear and his blowpipe was too short. He returned from the forest with nothing to eat.

The animals were no longer his friends. Word went round the forest: 'Man is a hunter. Keep away from him.' If Man ever entered the forest the birds would send warning messages to the other animals. They screamed, sang or called to each other: 'Man is a hunter. Keep away.'

Man the hunter was alone. He had no friends. He knew the animals hated him now. Even if he went to the forest without his weapons, he could sense their mistrust of him. They stopped screaming, calling or singing. All he could hear was their silence. He was frightened to return to the forest. He needed a friend. So he prayed for an animal that would be his friend. Then, one day, in his search for food, he went down to the river to catch some fish. He sat on a log with his feet in the water, but there were piranha fish in the river with razor-like teeth, so he decided to make himself a canoe. Sitting in his canoe, Man could fish in the middle of the river. Every day Man fished and every evening he returned laden with lots of fish, which he roasted on a wood-fire.

But God was not pleased that Man was taking all the fish from the river. 'If this fishing goes on, there will be no fish left!' he said to himself. 'I will give Man a companion to go with him in the forest, to help him find the hiding places of the forest animals, and to keep watch over him at night. Then he will leave the river and go back to the forest.'

That night, after God had finished his work in the sky, he went to the wood-fire where all the fish were laid out — all different colours, shapes and sizes. He took each fish in turn and moulded it into the shape of a dog. He gave legs to the body, and moulded the head of each fish into the head of a dog; some with narrow heads, some with wide heads, dogs of all shapes and sizes, just as they are today, and some just like me. The part of the head that God held in his hand became the nose, but it remained cold.

'To this day there is a dog in every home, watching over families at night, tracking down animals for Man, and living with Man. And that is why every dog has a cold nose,' announced Dexter the Dog.

Ernest the Eagle

Ernest the Eagle had flown most of the way, all the way from Scotland in fact. But most nights, he had made camp with the other animals along the route. That particular night they were staying at Bar-sur-Aube in France, where many pilgrims throughout the centuries had stopped on their way to Rome to see the Pope. The animals were camping by the banks of the River Aube, and were looking forward to hearing the next story.

Ernest didn't want to show off and describe how wonderful eagles were, although secretly that's how he felt. However he decided to relate a story about why there is a reason for everything ...

Why the Eagle Nests in Winter

Jack the rabbit was being chased by an enormous eagle and so he fled as fast as he could to his burrow. On the way, however, he spied the nest of the beetle, his next-door neighbour. He decided that this was just as safe a place to hide.

'Nowhere safer than this,' he thought, as he lay snugly in the nest.

But he was wrong. The huge bird swooped down into the beetle's nest and seized poor Jack.

'Let me go, let me go,' screamed Jack the rabbit.

The beetle, whose home it was, had been watching this little scene, and tried to intercede for her friend, the rabbit: 'O Eagle, Queen of Birds, I know that you can easily carry off poor Jack whenever you please. But he's pleading for his life. Please show some mercy and let him go! Save him or kill us both — he is both my neighbour and my friend.'

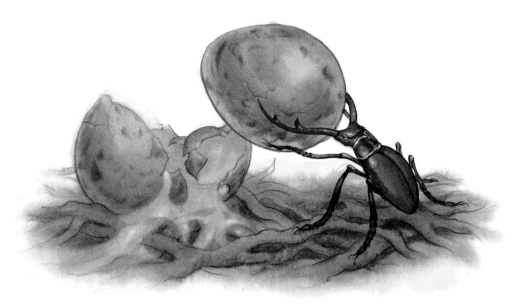

The eagle would soon have babies to feed and took no notice of this entreaty. She flapped at the beetle with her wings and the beetle became too frightened to speak again. The eagle rose with Jack the rabbit up into the sky.

The beetle was very angry at this behaviour, and rushed to the nest of the absent eagle. The beetle was in such a terrible rage that she crushed all the lovely delicate eggs that the eagle had laid — every single one of them.

The eagle returned home to her devastated nest and screamed and screamed as loud as loud could be. And worst of all, she did not know who had done this terrible deed. She roamed around the skies crying and sadly lamenting her lost babies.

The following year, the eagle decided to build her nest even higher up in the trees. She thought it would be safer, but the beetle was still out for vengeance and after crawling up the tree, she smashed all the eggs inside the nest, avenging the death of Jack the rabbit yet again.

The eagle mourned her loss even more greatly than the first time. She shrieked and shrieked and kept all the animals in the woods awake for many days and nights.

The year after, she decided to go and ask for God's help. God lived high up in the mountains, but it did not take her long to fly there. She put her eggs into his lap, thinking nothing could disturb them there. They remained there safely and soundly and God kept them warm and protected.

But the beetle discovered what the eagle had done and she changed her tactics, like any other cunning enemy. So she also went up to God and threw some dirt on to his robes. While God was busy shaking all the dirt off, the eggs fell out of his lap.

When the eagle discovered what had happened, she was so angry, she said many cruel things to God. She threatened to leave God's kingdom, and said she would live wild in the desert. God smiled forgivingly at her, and then summoned the beetle to him. The beetle related all that had happened and God chastised the eagle for carrying off Jack the rabbit. But still the eagle and beetle continued to rage and argue. They just would not stop bickering with each other.

So in his wisdom, God decided to keep the eagle and the beetle apart. He therefore changed the time of the year when eagles could mate together. So now when the eagle lays her eggs, it is in the cold and dark days of winter. No beetles dare roam around in winter, and like moles they lie snug and sightless in their holes. It is far too cold for them to venture out, looking for eagles' nests.

'The eggs of the eagle are now safe and sound, and that is why the eagle nests in winter,' announced Ernest, earnestly.

Toto the Tortoise

Toto the Tortoise was not having trouble keeping up with the other animals.
Although tortoises were slow, they knew how to conserve their energy. Toto
didn't rush things, but she kept to a steady pace. She had come all the way from
Australia, so she was used to long journeys. Of course, she hadn't walked all the
way. She had been on a ship for many weeks, where one of the sailors on board
had fed her and kept her as a pet. She had joined some of the other animals at
the port of Calais. By now, the travellers had reached Besançon in the east of
France. Besançon, which is near Dijon, was set amongst undulating hills and
green valleys, and the brown hillsides were striped with vineyards.

It was now Toto the Tortoise's turn to tell a story. As usual she didn't rush.
She spoke evenly and clearly ...

How the Tortoise got its Shell

A very long time ago, all the Australian bush animals and birds lived in a huge deep valley, surrounded on every side by tall, craggy hills. There was hardly any food to eat so all the animals and birds got together and had a special meeting about this problem. How could they get hold of more food? They talked and talked for many hours, but nobody could come up with any suggestions.

At last the tortoise rose to speak. All the animals laughed. Everybody made fun of the tortoise, for he was so slow and clumsy. He was thought a fool, because he was either always asleep, or sleepy. However, the tortoise had an idea. He suggested that the big eagle, the king of all the birds, and a great hunter, should fly over the mountains and find food.

'Yes,' said the eagle. 'I will do that.' And away he flew.

When the eagle had flown a long way over the mountains, he saw a beautiful country full of all kinds of food, but he couldn't see any birds or animals there, except for one little bird called a white wagtail.

'My brothers and sisters are very hungry. Can they come to this beautiful country of yours?' he asked the wagtail.

'Oh yes,' replied the wagtail, 'but you must wrestle with me first.'

'This will be easy,' thought the eagle, but the clever little white wagtail had placed some large spiky fish-bones in the place where he said they would wrestle. When they began to tussle, the wagtail was very quick and nimble, and hopped and jumped about a lot. All of a sudden, the wagtail tripped up the eagle, who fell among the sharp fish spikes and was pinned to the ground. He was now at the mercy of the wagtail, who pecked him to death.

Meanwhile, all the other animals and birds in the valley over the mountains waited eagerly for the eagle to return. After a while, they grew tired of waiting, so they sent the hawk out instead.

Unfortunately, the hawk met the same fate as the eagle. Then they sent the magpie, the wombat, the dingo, the kangaroo and many others. But all in turn were tricked by the cruel little white wagtail. They all fell on the fish spikes, and were pecked to death. All the remaining birds and animals became very worried. Not one of the animals who had travelled over the mountains ever returned.

The situation was very serious. The animals and birds had to find food somewhere. Then the old tortoise volunteered to go. He went on his way very slowly, over the mountains and into the beautiful country where the white wagtail lived. As usual, the wagtail invited the visitor to wrestle.

'Of course, I'll wrestle you,' said the tortoise, 'but please wait just one minute.'

The tortoise went into the bush and cut a big boat-shaped piece of wood and a thick strip of bark from a gum tree. The tortoise placed the curved wood over his back and he tied the thick sheet of bark on to his chest to use as a breastplate. He was now ready to fight the white wagtail.

The quick and lively wagtail hopped round and round, and soon tripped up the slow old tortoise. But when the tortoise fell on the fish spikes, he was protected by the wood and the bark. The wagtail tripped the tortoise again and again, but every time he was saved either by the wood on his back, or by his bark breastplate. After a while, the white wagtail became exhausted, and the tortoise was able to catch and destroy the evil little bird.

Of course, the tortoise returned to his country as quickly as he could. He told all the other animals and birds where they could find food in the beautiful country. Where the eagle, hawk, dingo, kangaroo, and all the other animals had failed to succeed by force, the slow-moving old tortoise had managed to succeed with wisdom and cunning.

And to this day, every tortoise carries the boat-shape on his back — it is called a carapace — and it also wears a breastplate.

'The carapace is a reminder of the victory the tortoise had over an enemy. Throughout the long years of its life, a tortoise seeks to serve. It wears its shield with humility and never asks for praise,' said Toto solemnly.

Hari the Hare

The animals were now on their way to Lausanne in Switzerland. This part of the country was filled with neat rows of Swiss chalet houses with window boxes full of geraniums. In the distance the grey-green hills were getting steeper, and some even had snow on them.

Hari the Hare came from the north of Africa. He hadn't met the animals in Paris. He had come up through Spain and travelled all the way across France, from the west to the east. He met the animals when they arrived at Besançon. As he was such a fast runner, it hadn't taken much time to catch up with them.

Hari was not quite sure about this storytelling business, but he agreed to have a go. The hare sometimes gets confused with the rabbit and several tales about the hare have now become stories about the rabbit. The hare can be depicted in many ways and in many guises but Hari wanted to show that the hare has wisdom. His story was simply called:

The Hare is the Judge

Many years ago, there was an ape who was a hunter. One day, just as the hunter was going to take a pig and antelope out of his traps, a lion sprang out at the ape and with these words threatened to kill him: 'I will kill you, unless you give me a share of your meat.'

The ape was very frightened indeed, and so he agreed to the lion's request. He let the lion cut out the hearts, livers and whatever else he chose from the pig and the antelope. Then the miserable ape, in a sulky mood, carried the rest home.

This happened every day, and soon the ape's wife became very curious. All the animals that the ape carried home never had a heart or a liver. The wife became very jealous, and felt sure that her husband had given the hearts and the livers of all these animals to another female. The ape denied these accusations but she did not believe him.

One morning she got up very early and followed him to where he laid his traps. Unfortunately she tripped, and fell into one of the traps laid by her husband.

Soon the ape and the lion arrived at the scene, and just like every other day, the lion demanded his share. This meant the ape would have to kill his wife so he refused. But the lion insisted: 'You have to keep to your side of the bargain.'

The ape was desperate, and was just about to give in and kill his wife. The poor female was having to pay dearly for her suspicious mind, when luckily a hare happened to pass by near the trap and saw her lying there. The ape saw the hare and called out to him for his help: 'Oh, wise Mister Hare, please help us. We are in a very difficult situation.'

First, the hare said it was none of his business, but the ape continued to implore him.

And at last the hare yielded to the ape's entreaties. So he stopped still in his tracks and asked the ape and the lion to tell their sides of the story. After he had listened to both of them he ordered the ape to release his wife, and to set the trap again. The ape did this and then the hare asked the lion to show him how the wife had got into the trap.

The lion obliged and said: 'This is how it caught her.'

And indeed, the lion fell into the trap! The cunning hare had laid a trap in more ways than one! The lion was caught by his legs and couldn't move.

'Let me go, let me go!' he cried.

But the hare ignored the lion, and turned to the ape. He said: 'You were a great fool to make such a promise to the lion. Now be off with you and take your wife.'

The ape did not bother to be told twice and ran off home with his wife. The wife learned not to be jealous or suspicious ever again.

Meanwhile the lion had continued to call out: 'Please release me, release me, let me go!'

The hare thought about leaving him there, but eventually he set him free, and even gave him some of his own food. He wanted to show the lion that animals could be generous.

'So the little hare was always on good terms with his larger neighbours, the apes and the lions, and everybody thought he was rather a nice kind of animal,' said Hari with a smile.

Jack the Jackal

The animals had passed many lakes and gushing waterfalls. They were approaching the Alps, the biggest mountain range in Europe. The weather was getting colder and colder, and the snow on the mountain tops was getting thicker and thicker, when the animals decided to stop for the night.

It was now Jack the Jackal's turn to tell a story. Jack the Jackal had come all the way from India. He was not particularly impressed by the Alps. The Himalayas in Asia were so much bigger, but he didn't want to appear too superior. The jackal wasn't a very popular animal. Unlike the tortoise, jackals were not known for their humility, so Jack wanted to make a good impression with his story:

The Indigo Jackal

Once upon a time there was a jackal who lived in a forest. He liked prowling around the outskirts of the town. One night he accidentally fell into a huge tub of indigo, which was a blue dye. He could not get out of this tub, so he pretended to be dead and remained there until morning.

When the owner of the tub saw the jackal, he thought he was dead and so he lifted him out of the tub. He carried him some distance away and then threw him down to the ground. After a while, when the tub-owner had gone, the jackal ran off and went back to the forest. He then looked down at himself and realised that he was completely covered in blue.

He started thinking to himself: 'I am now blue, the very best of colours. I should do something with my life, better my position and all that.'

He considered the matter for a while, and then called all the jackals together for a meeting. When they had all arrived, he said to the assembled jackals: 'I have been blessed by God, as you can see for yourselves. I have been annointed with an essence of all the plants in the forest. Look at my colour. From this day, therefore, all the animals in the forest shall be under my command.'

The jackals saw that he was indeed a wonderful bright colour, and so they all bowed down to the ground and said: 'Your will is our command, your Majesty.'

So the jackal became the king of the forest and gradually gained power over all the other animals. He surrounded himself with a court of lions and tigers. He felt very regal and soon began to be embarrassed by other jackals — his own kin. They were not very beautiful and the other animals had always looked down upon them. He therefore decided to banish all jackals from the forest.

All the jackals were very despondent and did not want to leave the forest — their natural home. But one old jackal said to them: 'Do not despair. Even though we have been treated with contempt by this individual who does not know how to

behave himself, we do know his weaknesses. I have a plan which will bring about his downfall. All those lions and tigers are deceived by his colour. They do not realise that he is a jackal and they naturally accept him as a king. You must therefore act in such away so that he betrays himself. You must follow my plan, which I shall now describe to you.'

The old jackal explained that the plan was for the jackals to wait until evening when they would all let out a great howl near to where the king jackal was sitting on his throne.

'When he hears the howling sound he will be bound to yell out an answer, because he is still a jackal underneath all that ghastly blue. Indeed, people do say that it is very difficult to shake off one's true nature. If a dog were made king and became hungry, would he not start gnawing on a shoe, just like any normal dog?'

The jackals agreed, and carried out the plan. Sure enough, when twilight came, the indigo jackal heard their great howls, and he himself started to howl back. Immediately one of the tigers recognised him for what he really was, and the jackal himself was banished from the forest.

This is the fate of a fool who deserts his own side and joins the enemy.

'Once a jackal, always a jackal!' said Jack cheekily.

Peter the Porcupine

The animals had now reached Aosta on the Italian side of the Alps. The scenery was still very rugged, and there were still lot of houses with steeply sloping roofs to cope with the snow. It did not seem so neat and tidy as Switzerland. The weather was cold, but the sun was beginning to shine.

Peter the Porcupine was a large rodent covered in spines. Spines are like sharp hairs and are sometimes called quills. Peter had not enjoyed the bumpy crossing over the Alps from Switzerland into Italy. He was not used to such high mountains. But Hannibal the Elephant had carried him over the tallest mountains. His elephant hide was so tough, he hadn't even noticed Peter's quills. Well, elephants had some uses after all, didn't they?

Peter had come all the way from North America. In native American folklore the porcupine is often an adversary of the beaver, so Peter was anxious to show that porcupines, as well as beavers, could be useful.

The Porcupine at the Meeting
of the Wild Animals

A long time ago, a tribe of men lived in the prairies. These men were very clever and strong. They were good hunters and caught many animals. They went hunting the whole year round, and the animals were frightened for their lives.

Grizzly Bear decided to call a meeting of the wild animals at his house.

'These hunting people have put us in great danger. They chase us right into our dens,' he said. 'I suggest that we ask God to give us more cold in winter to keep the hunters in their own houses and out of our dens.'

All the large animals agreed, and Wolf said, 'Let's invite all the smaller animals — Porcupine, Beaver, Raccoon, Marten, Mink, and even the really small ones such as Mouse and the insects to join us — strength in numbers and all that.'

Next day, the large animals met on a wide prairie and called together all the small animals, even the insects. The huge crowd sat down, the small animals on one side of the plain, the large animals on the other. Panther, Black Bear, Wolf, Elk and Reindeer all attended the meeting.

Then the grizzly bear, who was the chief speaker, rose and said: 'Dear friends, you know how the humans hunt us, over the hills and the mountains, even into our own dens. Therefore, my brothers and sisters, we large animals have asked God to give our earth cold winters, so that the people will be too cold to come and hunt us in wintertime. Is this not so, large animals?'

The panther said: 'I agree with this wise advice,' and all the other large animals said that they agreed.

Grizzly Bear then turned to the small animals and said: 'We want to know what you think of this matter.'

The small animals did not reply at first. After they had been silent for a while, Porcupine rose and said: 'Friends, let me say a few words in reply. Your plan is very good for you, because all of you have plenty of warm fur to keep you warm in winter. But look at these little insects. They have no fur to keep out the cold. How can insects and small animals keep warm if the winters are colder? So I say to you, don't ask for any more cold,' and with that he sat down.

Grizzly Bear then rose again: 'We do not need to pay attention to what Porcupine says,' he said to the large animals. 'You all agree, don't you, that we should ask for the most freezing cold on earth for winter?'

The large animals all replied: 'Yes, and we do not agree with Porcupine.'

So Porcupine rose again and said: 'Now, listen once more. I will ask you just one question. If it's that cold, the roots of all the wild berries will freeze and die, and all the plants of the prairies will wither away. How will you get food? You large animals always roam the mountains looking for something to eat. If you ask for more winter frost, you will soon die of hunger in the spring or summer. But we small animals will be more likely to survive — we can live on the bark or the gum of the trees, and the insects find their food in the soil.'

After he had made his speech, Porcupine put his thumb in his mouth and bit it off.

'Dash it all,' he said, and threw his thumb out of his mouth to show the large animals how brave he was. He sat down again, full of anger at the large animals. And so it is that the hand of the porcupine has only four fingers and no thumb.

The large animals were speech-

less. They had to admit that what Porcupine had said was right. Finally Grizzly Bear stood up and said: 'It is true what you say, Porcupine.' And so the large animals chose Porcupine as their wise man and the first among the small animals. Together all the animals agreed that there should be six months for winter, and six months for summer, the way it is now.

Then the wise Porcupine spoke again: 'In winter, we will have ice and snow. In spring we will have rain showers, and the plants will become green. In summer we will have warm weather, and all the fishes will go upriver. In the autumn, the leaves will drop, the rain will fall and the rivers and brooks will overflow. Then all animals, large and small, and insects who crawl on the ground, will go into their dens and hide for six months.'

All the animals agreed to what Porcupine had proposed, and happily, they returned to their homes.

That's why wild animals, large and small, take to their dens in winter. 'Only Porcupine does not hide, but goes about visiting his neighbours,' said Peter proudly.

Freda the Fox

Freda the Fox was enjoying herself immensely. She had never travelled so far before but she loved the mountain scenery. Now the travellers were entering the misty flat lands of the Po Valley. The animals were heading for the medieval city of Pavia, which was near Milan. Pavia was on the River Ticino which flows from Switzerland into the River Po. The snow-capped Alps lay behind the animals and in front of them were the blue of the Apennines. In the hazy distance a church could be seen.

Freda thought Pavia looked interesting, but she was really looking forward to reaching the shrine of St Francis. As a fox, Freda could never quite understand why foxes had such a bad reputation — they never got a good press. And if you got her on to the subject of fox-hunting, she'd never stop. In fact, she usually went on demonstrations against fox-hunting rather than pilgrimages. So this was a nice change, and she wanted to show that foxes could be helpful — sometimes ...

The Fox and the Horse

There was once a peasant farmer who had a very faithful horse. The horse had laboured for years and years, but was now too old to work. His master decided he could no longer afford to feed him, and one morning he said to him: 'I have a problem. You are no longer of any use to me. But I don't want to be unfair to you. If there's still some strength left in you, bring me a lion and I will continue to feed you.'

The peasant drove the horse out of his stable, and said: 'Now get out, and see what you can do'.

With that, he drove the horse into an open field, and wouldn't let him return. The poor old horse felt very sad and dejected. He didn't know where to go, but eventually decided to head in the direction of the wood to seek shelter from the cold weather.

In the wood, he happened to meet a fox. The fox saw the sorry-looking horse and asked him: 'What's up? Why are you hanging your head and wandering

around in this aimless way?'

'Ah,' cried the horse. 'My cruel master has forgotten how loyal I have been to him in all my years, working from morning till night. Because I am now too old to plough, he will no longer feed me, and he has driven me out.'

'Just like that — without saying anything else?' inquired the fox.

'Only saying that if I am strong enough, I should bring him home a lion, and he will continue to keep me. But he knows perfectly well that I can't possibly carry home a lion. I am too old and too weak.'

So the fox thought about this a little, and then said: 'Well now, maybe I can help you out of your difficulty. Lie down, stretch yourself out to full length, and pretend to be dead.'

The horse did as he was told, and laid down, pretending to be dead. The fox went off in search of the lion, whose den was not far from the wood.

'Come,' he said to the lion, 'there's a horse lying dead in the wood, and you can have a good square meal out of it if you like.'

The lion could not believe his luck, and immediately accompanied the fox back to the wood. When they were standing over the horse, the fox said: 'I've been

thinking, it won't be very comfortable for you to eat your lunch here. Let me tie the dead animal to your tail, and then you can drag him back to your den and eat to your heart's content, in peace and privacy.'

The lion decided this was a very good suggestion, and stood quite still so that the horse could be fastened to his tail. But instead of doing this, the fox tied the lion's legs to the horse's tail. He managed to do this so quickly and securely, that there was no way the lion could untie the knot. When he had finished his nimble work, he tapped the horse on the shoulder and said: 'Run, champion, run!'

In an instant, the horse sprang to his feet and bounded off, dragging the lion with him. The lion roared and bellowed, frightening all the birds in the process, but the horse let him roar and never stopped going until he arrived at his master's door.

The old peasant could not believe his eyes when he saw the horse with the lion, but he kept his promise and allowed the horse to stay with him. The horse was well-fed and content until the end of his days.

'So foxes can be helpful sometimes,' mused Freda.

Charlie the Coyote

The animal pilgrims were climbing across the Apennine hills into the west side of Italy and they decided to stop at Castelletto, a tiny little village high in the hills for the night.

Charlie the Coyote looked like a big dog or wolf. He was very intelligent and very fast. He had come all the way from North America.

There are many native American stories about the Coyote, who is always described as being very cunning and tricky. Charlie did not know which story to choose. There were so many. He didn't want to sound too full of himself and he thought the other animals would like to hear something quite unusual ...

The Coyote Dances with a Star

God gave the Coyote great intelligence, and because of this Coyote thought he was very powerful and he became rather conceited. Coyote thought that there was nothing he could not do. Sometimes he even thought he was more powerful than God. So Coyote was sometimes wise, but also a fool. God had also given Coyote three lives, but Coyote did not realise this.

One day, a long time ago, Coyote decided he wanted to dance with a star.

'I really feel like dancing with a star,' he said to himself.

He saw a bright star coming up from behind a mountain and called out: 'Hey, you star, come down. I want to dance with you.'

So the star descended and Coyote grabbed hold of him. But then the star soared up into the sky, with Coyote hanging on for dear life. Round and round the sky they went. Coyote became very tired, and his arm, which was holding on to the star, grew very numb. It felt as if it was coming out of its socket.

'Star,' he said. 'I think I've done enough dancing for now. I'll let go now and get back home.'

'No, wait,' said the star. 'We're too high up. Wait until I come lower over the mountain where I picked you up.'

Coyote looked down at the earth. He thought it looked quite near. 'I think I'll leave now, we're low enough,' he said. And with that, he let go.

Coyote had made a bad mistake. He dropped down and fell and fell and fell. He fell for a full ten winters. He ploughed through the clouds and when he finally hit the ground, he was flattened out like a stretched bearskin. And he died right there and then.

But, as I said, God had given Coyote more than one life. But it took Coyote quite a few years to pump himself up again into his old shape. He had grown quite old by this time, but he was still just as foolish.

'Who but me can dance with the stars, and fall out of the sky for ten long winters, and live to tell the tale? I am Coyote. I am the powerful one. I can do anything I want,' he boasted.

One night Coyote was sitting outside his lodge when he saw a very strange star coming from behind the mountain. It was a very fast star, with a long, trailing and shiny tail.

'What a fast star!' exclaimed Coyote. 'Wouldn't it be fun to dance with him. Hey, strange star with the long tail,' he called out. 'Wait for me, come down and let's dance!'

The fast star shot down, and Coyote caught hold of him. The star whirled off into the dark, vast universe. Again Coyote had made a bad mistake. When he had looked up from his lodge into the sky, he had had no idea of the star's real speed. It was the fastest thing in the universe. It whirled Coyote round so quickly, that first one and then his other leg dropped off. Bit by bit other parts of Coyote's body were torn off, until at last only Coyote's right hand was holding on to the fast star.

Coyote fell down to earth in little pieces, which scattered all over the place. But soon the pieces started looking for each other, and slowly they came together, and formed up into Coyote again. This took a long time and several winters passed. But at last Coyote was whole again. Except for his right hand, that is, which was still whirling round in space with the star. Coyote realised that he was a big fool.

'Dear God, I was wrong,' he cried. 'I am not as powerful as you. I'm not as powerful as I thought. Have pity on me.'

Then God spoke: 'Friend Coyote, I have given you three lives. You have already wasted two very stupidly. So be very careful now with your last one.'

Coyote replied, 'I will, God, and have pity on me. Please give me back my right hand.'

'That's up to the fast star with the long tail, my friend,' replied God. 'You must be patient. Wait until the star reappears, and rises from behind the mountain again. Then maybe he will shake your hand off.'

'How often does the fast star come over the mountain?' asked Coyote.

'Once every one hundred years,' said God.

'And so the Coyote had to wait one hundred years before the fast star gave him back his right hand,' said Charlie quietly.

Mango the Monkey

Some days later, the pilgrims made camp on the rocky Mediterranean coast, quite near the marble quarries of Carrara in Tuscany. The animals were enjoying being by the sea, the skies were blue and it was warm. It was time for another story.

Mango the Monkey had travelled all the way from China. He and most of his relatives were followers of Buddha, which meant they were Buddhists. Mango had joined the pilgrimage out of curiosity, as he was interested in all religions.

Mango had already told the other animals on the pilgrimage that there is a Chinese legend that Buddha invited all animals to come and visit him.

However only twelve of the animals, including the monkey, accepted Buddha's invitation to come and see him. So as a reward, Buddha gave each animal a year. So it is that in Chinese astrology each year has an animal sign, and the monkey is one of them.

Monkeys are very curious, intelligent and try to make the best of any situation. They are quick-witted and never at a loss for words. Mango, who had all of these characteristics, decided to tell the following story.

The Monkey Fools the Dragon

Once upon a time, there was an old dragon living in the sea and his wife was not feeling very well. She looked very pale and sad, so the dragon asked her if she wanted anything to eat. Mrs Dragon pulled her mouth shut and did not say a word.

'Just tell me, and I will get you anything you want,' pleaded Mr Dragon.

'Well, you can't get what I want, so why bother?' sighed Mrs Dragon.

'Trust me, and you shall get your wish,' said Mr Dragon, calmly.

'Well, I want a monkey's heart to eat,' stated Mrs Dragon, curtly.

'But the monkeys live miles away in the mountain forests! How can I get you a monkey's heart?' wondered Mr Dragon.

'Well, if I don't get one, I shall die, I know I shall,' cried Mrs Dragon.

56

So the dragon went up on to the beach and started climbing up the mountain towards the forest. And after many hours, he came across a monkey at the top of a tree.

'Hello, little one, aren't you afraid that you might fall?' the dragon asked the monkey high up in the tree.

'No,' replied the monkey, 'I'm not afraid I might fall.'

'Why do you eat from only one tree?' asked the dragon. 'If you cross the sea, you will find forests full of different fruit and flowers.'

'But how can I cross the sea?'

asked the monkey, as he started to think about lots of lovely different fruit and flowers.

'Get on my back, and I will take you over the sea,' ordered the dragon. So the monkey climbed down from the tree and hopped on the dragon, and after a long journey, the dragon arrived at the sea. Suddenly the dragon, with his tiny load on his back, dived into the sea.

'What did you do that for?' asked the monkey, his eyes and mouth full of salt water. The dragon continued to dive downwards. 'Where are we going now?' the monkey cried.

'Oh, my dear little monkey,' replied the dragon. 'I am taking you to my wife. She is very sad and ill, and has taken a fancy to your heart.'

'What shall I do?' thought the monkey. He had to think of something fast. Then he spoke: 'Dear friend, why didn't you tell me this in the first place? I've left my heart at the top of the tree. Take me back and I will get it for your wife, Mrs Dragon.'

So the dragon returned to the shore with the monkey on his back. After many hours of travelling, the monkey climbed up the same tree as before. A little while later, the dragon said: 'Hurry up, little friend, I am waiting.'

And the monkey thought to himself: 'What a fool this dragon is!'

Suzi the
Spider

The animals had passed through Florence and were now in the beautiful city of Siena. Siena's stunning cathedral has a white and green-patterned marble facade. The horses in the party were interested to see Siena. They had heard this was where the famous horserace around the main square took place every summer — it was called the Palio.

Suzi the Spider had been very lucky on the journey, getting lifts from lots of different animals. Unlike humans, none of the animals seem to be scared of her. In fact, she felt rather small and inconspicuous surrounded by all the other larger creatures, but she was determined to tell a story too. In traditional African and West Indian folklore, spiders live by their wits, but Suzi wanted to tell a story to show that spiders don't always come out on top.

The Spider and the Turtle

Spider was always hungry and was always eating. He was greedy too, and always wanted more than his share of things. So the other animals kept well clear of Spider.

But one day, a stranger came to Spider's home in the bush. His name was Turtle. Turtle was a long way from home. He had been walking all day in the hot sun, and he was very tired and hungry. So Spider felt he had to invite Turtle into his house for something to eat. He didn't really want to do this, but it was the local custom. If word got round that he hadn't been hospitable to a traveller, then the other animals would start talking about him behind his back.

So he said to Turtle: 'There is water in the spring where you can wash your feet. Follow the track, and you'll come to it. While you're doing that, I'll get the dinner ready.'

Turtle waddled down to the spring as quickly as he could, which in fact, was quite slowly. He dipped his feet into the spring and carefully washed his feet. Then he waddled back up the track to Spider's house. But the track was dusty. By the time Turtle got back to the house, his feet were covered in dirt again.

Spider had all the food set out. The table looked a picture. The smell of food made Turtle's mouth water. He was starving — he hadn't eaten since dawn. But Spider looked with disapproval at Turtle's feet.

'Your feet are very dirty,' Spider said, with his head up in the air. 'Don't you think you should wash them before you start to eat?'

Turtle looked at his feet and was ashamed they were so dirty. So he turned round and waddled back down to the spring again. He washed his feet once more, very carefully. Then he hurried as fast as he could back to the house. But as we know it takes a turtle a long time to go anywhere. By the time he arrived at the house, Spider had already started eating.

'Mm ... it's yummy this meal,' said Spider. He looked at Turtle's feet again. 'Hm, didn't you wash your feet, then?'

Turtle looked down at his feet. In his hurry to get back, he had stirred up a lot of dust on the track, and his feet were dirty again.

'I washed them. Washed them twice in fact,' sighed Turtle. 'It's that dusty track of yours that does it.'

'Oh,' said Spider. 'Now you're insulting my track, are you?' He took a big mouthful of food and munched it, looking very sulky.

'No,' said Turtle, by now quite exasperated. 'I was just trying to explain.'

'Well, go and get washed up so we can get on with our meal,' said Spider in a bossy way.

Turtle could see that the food was already half gone and Spider was eating as fast as he could. Turtle spun round and went off to the spring. He washed his feet and then instead of going back up the track, he walked on the grass and through the bushes. It took him a little longer, but at least his feet kept clean. When he got back to the house, Spider was licking his lips.

'Oh, what a lovely meal we had!'

Turtle looked at the dishes. Everything was gone. Even the smell. Turtle was so hungry, but he smiled and said: 'Yes, it was very good. You are very kind to travellers in your village. If you are ever in my country, you will always be welcome.'

'It's nothing,' said Spider sweetly.

Turtle went away. He didn't tell anyone about what had happened at Spider's house.

But one day many months later, Spider found himself a long way from home and in Turtle's country. He found Turtle on the lake shore, sunbathing.

'Hello, friend Spider,' said Turtle. 'You are a long way from your village. Will you come and have something to eat with me?'

'Yes, indeed — that's how it should be when someone is far from home,' said Spider. He was absolutely starving.

'Wait here on the shore,' said Turtle. 'I'll go below and prepare some food.' Turtle slipped into the water and went down to the bottom of the lake and set out some food to eat. Then he came back to the top of the lake and said to Spider, who was getting very impatient: 'Okay, everything is ready. Let's go down and eat.' Turtle put his head under the water and swam down.

Spider tried to follow Turtle. But he was too light. Every time he tried to dive, he floated. He splashed and splashed, kicked and kicked. But he always stayed on top of the water. For a long time he tried to get to the bottom, but he couldn't.

After a while Turtle came up, licking his lips.

'What's the matter with you, aren't you hungry?' he asked Spider. 'The food is delicious. You'd better hurry.' And back down he went.

Spider was desperate and so very, very hungry. He made one more attempt, but he still just floated. Then he had an idea. He went back to the shore, and picked up some pebbles. He put as many pebbles as he could in his pockets. Now he was really heavy. Then he jumped into the water again, and this time he sank to the bottom. There he found Turtle eating, and the food half gone. Spider couldn't wait to eat and was just reaching out to the food when Turtle said very politely: 'I beg your pardon, my friend, but in my country we never eat with our jackets on. Please take your coat off so that we can get down to eating.'

Turtle took a great mouthful of food. There was hardly any left. Spider was aching with hunger. So he wriggled out of his coat and grabbed at the food. But without the pebbles he was so light that he popped right back up to the top of the water.

'So do not try and trick anyone. They will always get their own back on you in the end,' said Suzi sagely.

William the Wolf

The animals were now very close to their destination. The sun was shining on the valleys filled with olive groves and the hills lined with cypress trees. They had already passed the multi-towered town of St Gimignano, and the hilltop town of Assisi could be seen high up in the distance.

There was a wolf on the pilgrimage. His name was William. He looked rather fierce but he was an old softy really. He said that as they were so close to Assisi now, he would tell a story about St Francis of Assisi.

The Wolf and St Francis of Assisi

St Francis of Assisi is the patron saint of animals. He was the son of a rich merchant. When he was young he enjoyed having fun and luxuries, but he had no sense of purpose or meaning to his life. So he changed his ways. Wearing the clothes of a pilgrim, he gave up his riches and visited the sick. He believed that being poor was the way to God. He started an order of monks, now called the Franciscans. The monks were known for their poverty and love of nature.

In paintings, St Francis is often seen preaching to insects, birds such as falcons, nightingales, swallows, and rabbits and even wolves, like myself.

Once, there was a very huge and ferocious wolf which roamed the countryside around Assisi. It was always very hungry and ate men, women and children as well as animals. But the wolf was not very happy with his life, and felt himself to be very lonely.

The people of Assisi were afraid to go into the country because of the wolf. If they did have to venture outside the city, they took guns with them. The city gates were closed so that the wolf could not get inside the city. St Francis decided to meet the wolf. He was not afraid of him. Nor was he afraid of the lions and snakes he passed on his way out of the city.

When St Francis came face to face with the wolf, the unhappy animal rushed against him. St Francis made the sign of the cross. The wolf was so surprised, he stopped in his tracks. St Francis closed the wolf's wide open mouth with his hands, and said: 'Come to me, brother wolf, and in God's name, I command you not to harm me or anybody.'

The wolf felt very humbled. He lowered his head and like a lamb lay down at the feet of the saint. St Francis stroked the wolf like a baby, and then the saint took the wolf back to the city. St Francis told the people that the wolf had promised that he would no longer harm any human or any animal. The wolf lifted his right paw, as if to give his promise, in front of the whole crowd.

In return the people promised to feed him. 'From then on the wolf was contented, and lived a good and happy life,' said William softly.

The storytelling had come to an end and all the animals were very happy that they had arrived at the place where their favourite saint was laid to rest. They made their way to the statue of Saint Francis. The animals all started singing hymns to thank God that they had all arrived at their destination safely.

GEOFFREY CHAUCER

Geoffrey Chaucer was born in around 1340 and died in the year 1400, so this book not only celebrates the millennium, but also commemorates the 600th anniversary of Chaucer's death. He is one of England's greatest poets. The Canterbury Tales, which is about a group of pilgrims who tell stories on their way to Canterbury, is his most famous work.

Chaucer worked as an administrator and diplomat at the court of King Edward III, and later at the court of his son, Richard II, and then Henry IV. Chaucer travelled widely in Europe, was familiar with Latin, French and Italian, and was greatly influenced by the literature written in these three languages, which he often translated into English.

He read his poetry at court, and was a very popular and successful civil servant. He was the first poet to be buried at Poet's Corner in Westminster Abbey.

About the Stories

Many stories crop up around the world in different versions and depicting different animals. Many animal myths and fables originated in Western Africa, from where they spread to Egypt, Greece, North America and even Australia. Some show animals in a positive light, some describe rivalry between animals, and others reveal how animals are either wiser or more stupid than tradition allows. Some stories have a moral, some relate why animals have certain characteristics or habits, and others describe how different cultures have been influenced by animals.

The Cat and the Mouse set up House

Cats and mice are very traditional rivals who were not meant to be friends. This story is taken from the collection by Jakob and Wilhelm Grimm called Grimm's Fairy Stories, which was originally published in German in 1819. The brothers Grimm wrote many animals stories but are more famous for writing fairy tales such as Cinderella, Sleeping Beauty, and Snow White.

A Dog's Nose is Cold

The dog is a man's best friend and this story explains why. It comes from the West Indies, and like many animal stories around the world, is a tale about some characteristic or attribute of an animal. This version is adapted from Philip Sherlock's collection, published by Oxford University Press in 1966.

Why the Eagle Nests in Winter

Eagles did not always nest in winter, but God decided to change the season. This story comes from Fables by the Frenchman Jean de La Fontaine, published between 1668-94. It was translated into English in verse form by Robert Thompson, in 1806. Many of La Fontaine's stories originally came from the Greek classic, Aesop's Fables, and consquently he gives animals many human characteristics.

How the Tortoise got its Shell

Traditionally, the tortoise is slow and has no outstanding talent, but as in Aesop and African tales, the tortoise is much cleverer than we think, and always manages to outwit his adversary. This story is adapted from the myths and legends of the Australian Aboriginals, retold by William Ramsay Smith in 1930.

The Hare is the Judge

The hare is considered to be wise, although he is not always so positively described – as in this story, which comes from Africa and was written down by Alice Werner in 1933. The hare is a favourite in the Bantu language, which is spoken from west to east in the sub-Saharan region. There are many versions of this story, including one from Zimbabwe. The hare often gets confused with the rabbit and is the origin of Brer Rabbit.

The Indigo Jackal

This story originated in India, where, as in Africa, jackals and hyenas are very popular, although they are laughed at rather than sympathised with. This story was adapted from the J.E.B. Gray collection published by Oxford University Press in 1961. It is taken from the Hitopadesha, a collection of Indian fables mostly about how the animal kingdom was organised and the wisdom of animals.

The Porcupine at the Meeting of the Wild Animals

Along with the bear and the beaver, the porcupine is very important to many American Indian tribes. Normally the beaver is the hero, with the porcupine as its enemy. This story is adapted from a collection of American Indian Myths and Legends, retold by Richard Erdoes and Alfonso Ortiz and published by Pantheon in 1984. It was originally narrated by Franz Boas of the Tsimshian tribe in 1916.

The Fox and the Horse

Although the fox is traditionally thought of as a sly and cunning creature, this story shows the fox in a much more kindly and sympathetic light. This version is adapted from the brothers Grimm, but needless to say, the fox appears in many stories from around the world.

The Coyote Dances with a Star

The coyote is one of the most important mythical characters in native American culture. He has many irritating qualities, but he is very much part of the creation myths popular with many tribes. This story is also adapted from American Indian Myths and Legends (as above), and is a compilation of various fragments told by the Cheyenne tribe.

The Monkey Fools the Dragon

The monkey is very important in Chinese mythology and was worshipped as a god. This animal is often given human attributes, and in this version, it is Buddha who plays the part of the monkey. The story is a Buddha myth and is based on a Chinese myth from a collection of Myths and Legends of China, told by Edward T. C. Werner in 1922.

The Spider and the Turtle

In the Ashanti language spoken in Ghana in West Africa, the spider is called Ananse. The Anansi stories originated in Africa and then travelled to the West Indies. In this story, the slow turtle turns the tables on the spider, who is usually depicted as a clever trickster. It also shows how cleanliness is very important to the Ashanti. This version is adapted from a story told by the Ashanti people and retold by Harold Courlander in 1947.

The Wolf and St Francis of Assisi

As the book is about a pilgrimage dedicated to St Francis of Assisi, this is the only story where a human, rather than an animal plays the most important role. It describes St Francis, who had great sympathy and power over many animals. The story is taken from The Little Flowers of St Francis, a version of which was published in English in 1883.

Lond